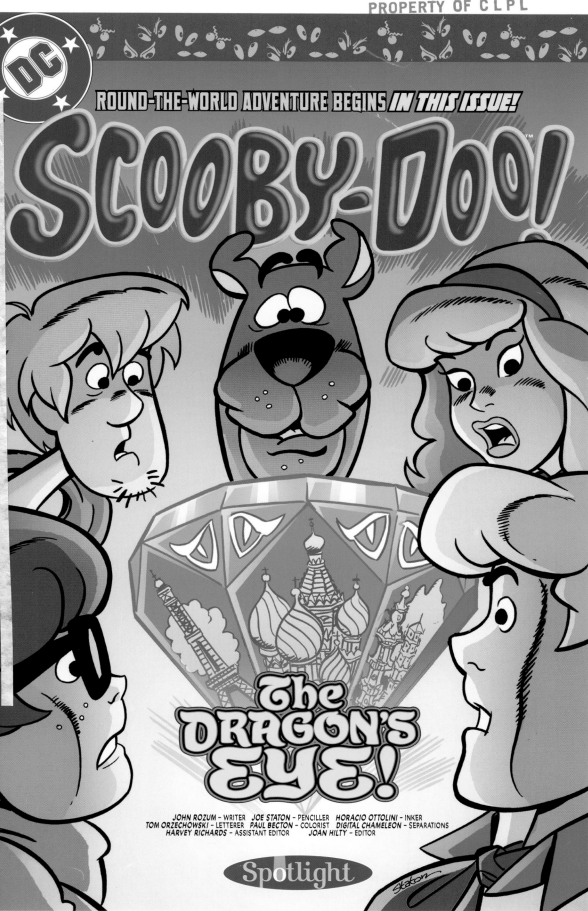

ROUND-THE-WORLD ADVENTURE BEGINS *IN THIS ISSUE!*

SCOOBY-DOO!

The DRAGON'S EYE!

JOHN ROZUM – WRITER   JOE STATON – PENCILLER   HORACIO OTTOLINI – INKER
TOM ORZECHOWSKI – LETTERER   PAUL BECTON – COLORIST   DIGITAL CHAMELEON – SEPARATIONS
HARVEY RICHARDS – ASSISTANT EDITOR   JOAN HILTY – EDITOR

Spotlight

VISIT US AT
www.abdopublishing.com

Reinforced library bound edition published in 2010 by Spotlight, a division of the ABDO Group, 8000 West 78th Street, Edina, Minnesota 55439. Spotlight produces high-quality reinforced library bound editions for schools and libraries. Published by agreement with Warner Bros.—A Time Warner Company. All rights reserved. Used under authorization.

Printed in the United States of America, North Mankato, Minnesota.
092009
012011

 PRINTED ON RECYCLED PAPER

Library of Congress Cataloging-in-Publication Data

Rozum, John.
  Scooby-Doo in The dragon's eye / writer, John Rozum ; penciller, Joe Staton ; inker, Horacio Ottolini ; colorist, Paul Becton ; letterer, Tom Orzechowski. -- Reinforced library bound ed.
     p. cm. -- (Scooby-Doo graphic novels)
  ISBN 978-1-59961-688-9
  I. Staton, Joe. II. Scooby-Doo (Television program) III. Title. IV. Title: Dragon's eye.
  PZ7.7.R69Sc 2010
  741.5'973--dc22
                                        2009031340

All Spotlight books have reinforced library bindings and
are manufactured in the United States of America.

MERCI.

WHAT IS IT, VELMA?

WE'VE BEEN INVITED TO A PARTY!

"AN INFORMAL GATHERING OF MYSTERY WRITERS, READERS, AND SOLVERS, HOSTED BY MADAME LeROUX, PATRONESS OF THE ARTS."

THAT SOUNDS LIKE FUN!

LIKE, IF YOU ASK ME, IT SOUNDS A LITTLE TOO RITZY. ANYWAY, I THOUGHT WE WERE ON VACATION TO GET AWAY FROM MYSTERIES?

OH, SHAGGY. WE'RE NOT BEING ASKED TO SOLVE ANYTHING!

IT'LL BE A GREAT WAY TO MEET SOME NEW PEOPLE. BESIDES, I'M SURE THE OTHER GUESTS WOULD BE THRILLED TO HEAR ALL ABOUT THE CASES YOU TWO BRAVELY SOLVED.

FREDDIE, YOU MUST BE THINKING OF SOMEONE ELSE--

--BECAUSE IF THERE'S ONE WORD SCOOBY AND I DON'T KNOW THE MEANING OF, IT'S "BRAVE"!

I CAN THINK OF ANOTHER WORD THAT MIGHT CONVINCE YOU TO GO--

--"HORS D'OEUVRES."

OUR FAVORITE FRENCH WORD! I'LL GET MY COAT!

ROOBY ROOBY ROO!

LATER...

KRAKADOOM

JINKIES, WHAT A *GREAT* APARTMENT!

YEAH-- USUALLY, WHEN WE'RE IN A PLACE LIKE THIS, IT'S COVERED IN COBWEBS, THE EYES IN THE PAINTINGS *MOVE*, AND SOME *CRAZY GHOST* IS CHASING US!

SCOOBY-DOO IN THE DRAGON'S EYE

PART 1: HOUSE OF THE SEVEN GARGOYLES

JOHN ROZUM – WRITER   JOE STATON – PENCILLER   HORACIO OTTOLINI – INKER
TOM ORZECHOWSKI – LETTERER   PAUL BECTON – COLORIST   DIGITAL CHAMELEON – SEPARATIONS
HARVEY RICHARDS – ASSISTANT EDITOR   JOAN HILTY – EDITOR

ZOINKS!

ROWWW-OW!

KRK BOOM

WHAT IS IT? DID SOMEONE ELSE EAT THE LAST SHRIMP?

R-R-RONSTER!

MONSTER? WHERE?

OUT T-T-THERE, ON THE L-L-LEDGE! AND THERE WERE S-SEVEN MORE BEHIND IT!

ACTUALLY, THERE ARE ONLY SIX.

YOU MEAN THERE ACTUALLY *ARE* MONSTERS OUT THERE?

OF COURSE! PARIS IS *SWARMING* WITH THEM!

THEY'RE *GARGOYLES*-- ORNAMENTAL *STATUES*, MEANT TO DRIVE AWAY EVIL SPIRITS.

NEVER MIND THE EVIL SPIRITS, THEY ALMOST DROVE *ME* AWAY!

SEE, NOTHING TO BE AFRAID OF!

BUT ONE OF THEM WAS STARING IN AT US--NOT *OUT* LIKE THESE!

IT MUST HAVE BEEN A TRICK OF THE LIGHT.

SOME TRICK--

--'CAUSE I COULD HAVE *SWORN* THERE WERE SEVEN!

YOU MUST BE THE MEMBERS OF *MYSTERY INC.*

THAT'S RIGHT, AND YOU MUST BE MADAME LeROUX. THANK YOU FOR INVITING US TO YOUR PARTY.

AU CONTRAIRE, I SHOULD BE THANKING *YOU.* WHEN I FOUND OUT YOU WERE VISITING PARIS, I SIMPLY *HAD* TO INVITE YOU!

WELL, WE'RE GLAD YOU DID. WE'RE HAVING A LOT OF FUN!

EXCEPT FOR THE SCARE WITH THE GARGOYLE!

YOU'RE THE ONLY *REAL* MYSTERY INVESTIGATORS HERE THIS YEAR--EVERYONE ELSE IS EITHER A FAN OR AN AUTHOR.

SEE, THERE'S *DASHIELL CHANDLER, AGATHA SOTHEBY, SIR ARTHUR CONAN O'BRIEN,* AND *SUE GRIFFON.*

THE PROBLEM IS, WHAT AM I GOING TO DO WHEN I GET TO *X?* "*X IS FOR...*" WHAT?

THAT'S REALLY QUITE A GEMSTONE YOU HAVE THERE, MADAME LeROUX. IT ALMOST SEEMS TO *GLOW FROM WITHIN.*

YES, AND YET IT'S NEVER BEEN POLISHED, OR EVEN CUT INTO A GEM. IT'S A FAMILY HEIRLOOM PASSED DOWN FROM MY GRANDMOTHER.

I ONLY WEAR IT ONCE A YEAR, AT THIS PARTY.

NOW IF YOU'LL EXCUSE ME--IT SEEMS THAT GUEST IS VENTURING INTO AN *OFF-LIMITS AREA!*

WHAT'S *YOUR* PART IN ALL THIS?

I WAS JUST LOOKING FOR THE COATROOM. I...I WAS ONLY HOPING TO TUCK THE MANUSCRIPT OF MY MYSTERY NOVEL INTO A PUBLISHER'S POCKET!

SAY--THERE'S A *ROPE* AT THE OTHER END OF THE LEDGE!

AND *THERE'S OUR GARGOYLE!*

HE'S HEADING FOR THE *ROOF!*

I NEED SOME OF YOU TO GO TO THE UPPER FLOORS TO MAKE SURE IT DOESN'T TRY TO SNEAK BACK IN THROUGH A WINDOW.

SHAGGY, SCOOBY-- YOU TWO COME WITH ME TO THE ROOF!

I HAD A FEELING HE WAS GOING TO SAY THAT!

WOW, AN ACTUAL MYSTERY!

ARE YOU SURE? I THINK IT'S SOME SORT OF PARTY GAME!

CREAK

YOU DID WELL. YOU'LL FIND THE OTHER HALF OF YOUR *PAYMENT* IN THE LOCATION YOU SPECIFIED.

ZOINKS! IT'S COMING OUR WAY!

RAB HIM!

GRAB HIM, ME?! YOU GRAB HIM--- WHOA!

WHOA-WHOA-WHOA-WHOA!

OH, NO--HE'S GETTING AWAY!

THIS SHOULD STOP ME...

WHOA-WHOA-WHOA--

CLAAANGG

GOOD WORK, SHAGGY, YOU'VE GIVEN ME AN IDEA!

SPLOOSH

FROM THE JOURNAL OF VELMA DINKLEY.

JULY 25. WE HAVE TRAVELLED FROM *PARIS* TO *MOSCOW*, WHERE WE ARE STAYING WITH *YURI AND TATIANA DRUZHKOV*.

THE DRUZHKOVS ARE GENEROUS HOSTS, AND THEY SEEM ENDLESSLY ENTERTAINED BY TALES OF OUR ADVENTURES.

THEY ARE INTRIGUED BY OUR MOST RECENT CASE. THE CASE THAT ALL BUT ONE OF US ARE WILLING TO LEAVE TO THE PARIS POLICE.

IT WAS ALL WE COULD DO TO DRAG FREDDIE OUT OF PARIS. THE FACT THAT THIS IS OUR ONLY UNSOLVED CASE SEEMS TO WEIGH HEAVILY ON HIM.

... I HAVEN'T *GIVEN UP* ON FINDING THE NECKLACE AND THE MASTERMIND BEHIND ITS THEFT!

BUT NO MATTER WHERE WE GO, IT NEVER TAKES LONG FOR A MYSTERY TO FALL IN OUR LAP. MOSCOW WAS NO EXCEPTION.

THIS STOLEN NECKLACE... YOU SAY THE STONE WAS UNPOLISHED, YET SEEMED TO *GLOW*. WAS THE GLOW FROM *WITHIN*?

YES, AS IF A *LIGHT* WERE BEING BEAMED THROUGH IT.

HOW DID YOU KNOW?

I'D LIKE TO SHOW YOU AN HEIRLOOM, WHICH I PLAN TO PASS ON TO MY GRAND-DAUGHTER HERE, MARINA. IT'S A *FABERGÉ EGG*.

LIKE, AS LONG AS FABERGÉ IS RUSSIAN FOR *HARD-BOILED* OR *SCRAMBLED*, YOU CAN SHOW US ALL THE EGGS YOU WANT!

≥SLUURP!≤

WELL, NOT QUITE--SEE FOR YOURSELF, IT'S RIGHT THERE ON THE MANTLEPIECE!

OH, IT'S JUST A KNICKKNACK. SORRY, SCOOB.

To SAY SCOOBY-DOO AND SHAGGY WERE UNDERWHELMED WOULD BE AN UNDERSTATEMENT!

YOU DOOFUS, SHAGGY! DO YOU HAVE ANY IDEA WHAT THAT "KNICKKNACK" IS *WORTH*?

THESE EGGS WERE MADE IN THE 19th CENTURY BY THE FAMED JEWELER *PETER CARL FABERGÉ*, UNDER ORDERS FROM THE CZAR OF RUSSIA. THEY WERE ANNUAL EASTER PRESENTS TO HIS WIFE, CZARINA MARIA.

INCLUDING THIS ONE, ONLY *FORTY-FIVE* OF THE *FIFTY-SIX* EGGS ARE KNOWN TO STILL EXIST!

*F*REDDIE WAS THE FIRST TO NOTICE WHY MRS. DRUZHKOV WANTED US TO SEE THE EGG.

NOT ONLY THAT, VELMA...DID YOU NOTICE THE *STONES*?

THEY LOOK LIKE THEY'RE THE SAME TYPE OF STONE AS THE ONE SET IN MADAME LeROUX'S STOLEN NECKLACE!

WHAT *KIND* OF STONES ARE THEY--AND WHY AREN'T THEY CUT, OR POLISHED?

NO EXPERT THAT I'VE ASKED SEEMS TO *KNOW*...

BUT I DO!

EVERY ONE OF OUR CASES SEEMS TO HAVE SOME KIND OF *WEIRDO* IN IT.

WE'VE TANGLED WITH VAMPIRES, GHOSTS, ALIENS, MONSTERS, PHANTOMS-- YOU NAME IT. THIS TIME IT WAS...

ZOINKS! A WITCH!

NOT JUST ANY WITCH, MY PRECIOUS-- *BABA YAGA!*

SCOOBY-DOO IN THE DRAGON'S EYE

PART 2: RUSSIAN INTO DANGER!

JOHN ROZUM – WRITER
JOE STATON – PENCILLER
HORACIO OTTOLINI – INKER
TOM ORZECHOWSKI – LETTERER
PAUL BECTON – COLORIST
DIGITAL CHAMELEON – SEPARATIONS
HARVEY RICHARDS – ASS'T EDITOR
JOAN HILTY – EDITOR

NICE TRY, MY PRECIOUS, BUT YOU'LL HAVE TO BE QUICKER IF YOU WANT TO BEAT BABA YAGA!

MY GOSH-- A SECRET *STAIRCASE* BEHIND THAT *BOOKCASE!*

KKKRRFF

AND, LIKE, IF I EVER SEE THAT WITCH AGAIN, I'M GOING TO END UP A *BASKET CASE!*

WOW, FREDDIE...

I'M OKAY, DAPHNE.

VELMA, I WANT YOU TO GO WITH SHAGGY AND SCOOBY AND FOLLOW BABA YAGA.

FOLLOW HER? H-HOW ABOUT YOU GIVE US OPTION NUMBER *TWO,* FREDDIE?

OKAY, IF YOU DON'T WANT TO FOLLOW HER, YOU CAN COME WITH ME AND WAIT FOR HER TO COME OUT THE OTHER END!

RUH-UH, REDDIE, NO RANK YOU!

C'MON, VELMA, LIKE *LEAD THE WAY!*

YURI TOLD US THAT THE *TUNNEL* CAME WITH THE HOUSE--THAT IT WAS BUILT AS AN *ESCAPE ROUTE* DURING THE RUSSIAN REVOLUTION. IT RUNS ABOUT A QUARTER-MILE AND EXITS BENEATH A FOUNTAIN.

I WAS MORE INTERESTED IN WHY A *MYTHOLOGICAL CREATURE* HAD *DIESEL FUEL* LEAKING OUT OF HER FLYING MORTAR!

Hmmm.

MEANWHILE, THE OTHERS REACHED THE OTHER END OF THE TUNNEL.

I HOPE WE AREN'T TOO LATE!

THE TUNNEL IS DARK AND HAS A LOW CEILING-- HOPEFULLY IT SLOWED HER DOWN!

YURI, DO YOU REMEMBER WHERE THE DOOR IS?

YES, IT SHOULD BE ABOUT A FOOT TO YOUR--

≥UNGH≤

OUT OF MY WAY, OR I'LL GOBBLE YOU UP!

≥OOF≤

THE MORTAR, IT TURNED OUT, WAS A DRESSED-UP VERSION OF AN EXPERIMENTAL *HOVER-PLATFORM* DEVELOPED BY THE SOVIET MILITARY.

SKRTCCCH

OUR BABA YAGA TURNED OUT TO BE A FORMER KGB AGENT NAMED *IRINA MOLOTOVA.* SINCE T~~ FALL OF THE SO~~ EMPIRE, SHE'D~~ A LIVING AS~~ DEALER--AN~~

I WOULD HAVE GOTTEN AWAY WITH IT, IF IT WEREN'T FOR YOU *MEDDLING KIDS!*

MAN, OH, MAN, SCOOB. YOU'D BETTER WAIT FOR YOUR STOMACH TO STOP SPINNING BEFORE YOU EAT THAT SCOOBY SNACK!

BUT, WHERE'S MRS. DRUZHKOV'S *FABERGÉ EGG?*

GOOD JOB, SCOOBY--BUT PLEASE DON'T TELL ME YOU ATE THE *STONES!*

RUH-UH. RARE RID REY RO?

DON'T LOOK AT ME FOR ANSWERS. *HA-HA- HA-HA!*

TERRIFIC. NOW, POOR FREDDIE WAS REALLY PULLING HIS HAIR OUT. *TWO* CASES IN A ROW, *TWO* SIMILAR STONES, *TWO* THIEVES CAUGHT--

--BUT BOTH TIMES, THE STONES HAD *VANISHED!*

I MAY NOT HAVE KNOWN WHERE THEY'D GONE-- BUT THERE WAS *ONE* PART OF BOTH MYSTERIES I *KNEW* I COULD SOLVE.

ALL IT REQUIRED WAS A TRIP TO THE LIBRARY, SOME HELP TRANSLATING RUSSIAN, AND A LITTLE TIME ON THE INTERNET--

--AND I HAD MY *ANSWERS.*

NOW, ALL I HAD TO DO WAS TELL THE OTHERS.

FREDDIE, I THINK YOU'RE RIGHT. WE *CAN* SOLVE THESE TWO UNFINISHED MYSTERIES.

I EVEN KNOW *HOW.*

I TOLD THEM EVERYTHING I HAD LEARNED.

OVER A THOUSAND YEARS AGO, A MYSTERIOUS *GLOWING GREEN STONE* WAS UNEARTHED IN CHINA. WHEN THE STONE WAS PRESENTED TO THE EMPEROR, HE NAMED IT *"THE DRAGON'S EYE."*

THE DRAGON'S EYE WAS SAID TO CONTAIN *GREAT POWER*; POWER TO DEFEAT *ARMIES* OR TO OVERTURN AN *EMPIRE*.

FEARING THAT ITS POWER MIGHT FALL INTO THE WRONG HANDS, THE EMPEROR CUT THE STONE INTO *SEVEN* INTERLOCKING STONES.

THESE SEVEN SMALLER STONES HE DISTRIBUTED AMONG HIS *SEVEN SONS*.

OVER THE CENTURIES, THE STONES WERE SOLD OFF, TRADED, OR STOLEN FROM THE SONS, AND HAVE PASSED THROUGH MANY HANDS SINCE.

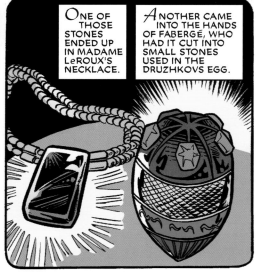

ONE OF THOSE STONES ENDED UP IN MADAME LeROUX'S NECKLACE.

ANOTHER CAME INTO THE HANDS OF FABERGÉ, WHO HAD IT CUT INTO SMALL STONES USED IN THE DRUZHKOVS EGG.

THE OTHER STONES ARE EITHER IN PRIVATE HANDS OR MUSEUM COLLECTIONS--

--SCATTERED ACROSS THESE *FIVE OTHER COUNTRIES*.

I THINK SOMEONE IS TRYING TO GATHER *ALL* THE STONES. UNTIL WE FIGURE OUT WHO THAT IS, I THINK OUR BEST BET IS TO STOP THE *NEXT THEFT!*

FREDDIE...I LEAVE IT TO YOU TO DECIDE WHICH OF THESE LOCATIONS WE SHOULD TRY NEXT.

GANG, PACK YOUR BAGS.

WE'RE GOING TO *ITALY!*

TO BE CONTINUED...